POISON DANCE

Livia Blackburne

Chapter One

IT WAS THE way she looked at James that caught his attention. The young woman didn't avoid his eyes like the serving lasses who hurried away after handing him his ale. Nor did she gaze at him coyly through her lashes like a dancer hoping for extra tips. This girl met his eyes straight on, and there was a quiet confidence in the way she held herself. She must have been watching James as he ate, because she came to him as soon as he stepped away from his table. She brushed her fingertips across his elbow.

"I would speak with you," she said, holding his gaze. The girl was tall, with auburn hair pulled back from a delicately featured face. She wore no makeup, and a loosely woven homespun dress hid her slight form from view. The skin of her hands and wrists was pale, almost translucent where they escaped her sleeves. She turned and walked away.

Despite her plain attire, the girl was attractive, and her request intriguing. James followed, though he did look back to make sure all was well at his table. Rand and Bacchus were engaged in a loud debate over which tavern had the best lamb stew. They hadn't yet noticed the girl.

She weaved gracefully between drunken revelers to a corridor that opened off the tavern's cask-lined back wall. The Scorned Maiden had filled up by now with after-supper patrons, and heat from the crowd made the air damp and heavy. James followed her halfway down the corridor's length

—far enough for them to be hidden in shadow but still within earshot of his companions. Then he stopped.

"We speak here," he said. Years in the Guild had taught him to take precautions.

She hesitated, glancing down the corridor in both directions. Then she slowly nodded. As she moved closer, he loosened the tie that bound one of his daggers to his arm. The knife dropped into his hand. The girl caught the glint of metal and flinched.

"Just being careful," he said, making no effort to sound reassuring.

She pulled her gaze away from his weapon and did a respectable job of wiping any fear from her face. When she spoke, her voice was cautious but steady. "I'm not foolish enough to lead you into a trap." Her speech lacked the rolling cadences common to Forge's peasants, but James couldn't place her accent.

Now that they were standing closer, he recognized her— the way she tilted her head and the graceful flow of her movements. Occasionally, her eyes caught the light from the dining room, and James saw that they were dark green. "You're one of the dancing girls." He hadn't recognized her without the costume and eye paint.

"And you're an assassin," she said.

He took his time answering. It was no secret that he was a member of the Guild, but it wasn't something usually announced on first meeting. "I may be."

"I would retain your services." Her tone was serious. She believed herself earnest, at least.

He gave a low chuckle. "Many think they would. But few have the coin, and even fewer truly have the stomach for it."

"I have enough coin."

"And how does a dancing lass come across so much money?" He dropped his eyes to her shapeless dress. "Unless your trade is not purely dancing."

She flushed now, her nervousness replaced with anger. "My business is my own. Will you take my coin or not?"

It raised his opinion of her, that she didn't meekly accept his insult. Nevertheless, he couldn't help her. "It doesn't work that way. I take orders from my guildleader."

"But do you have to? I could pay you well."

"I don't need the trouble."

The sounds of conversation in the dining room had died down, and James heard a talesinger's theatrical voice projecting over the crowd. He turned to leave, and she took his arm. "You have a job tomorrow, don't you?"

That stopped him. To know that he was in the Assassins Guild was one thing, but to know what he was doing the next day . . . "What of it?"

"If there's anything in your quarters you'd rather keep hidden, move it somewhere else before you leave. And you may want to return early."

He studied her face for any signs of deception. "I'll keep that in mind."

"And one more thing," she said before he could turn away again.

"What?"

"The rumors are right. Your guildleader is dead."

*   *   *

Bacchus wore a wide grin when James returned to the table. "Not bad. Though I didn't get a good look at her." His cheeks were red over his thick black beard.

"Couldn't, with that flour sack she was wearing," said Rand, scowling at his mug. While Bacchus could forget his troubles as soon as he entered a tavern, Rand didn't have that gift. And with rumors of the guildleader's death flying around, they'd had plenty to worry about.

"It was the redheaded dancer. The one who performed earlier today," said James.

Bacchus raised his eyebrows and peered over the crowd. "That was her? Lass must be blind. Or have a fancy for scarecrows." He gestured dismissively with a brawny arm toward James's lean form. James didn't bother to reply. Bacchus knew well enough that James could outfight him two times out of three.

"She told me Clevon's dead," said James.

That sobered even Bacchus up. "How does she know?"

"Says she overheard some men talking. Didn't know their names, but from her descriptions, it sounded like Gerred's crew."

Rand whistled darkly. "There'll be trouble if she's right."

The last time a guildleader had died was twenty years ago. Then, a much younger Clevon had fought his way to the top, leaving much of the existing Guild dead. It had been before James's time, but nothing he'd heard made him wish he'd been there. Across the table, Bacchus shifted, reaching for his weapons as if he expected assassins to materialize out of the walls.

James remained still, though it took some effort to suppress that same instinct to arm himself. "Gerred's firmly Clevon's second. Mayhap he'll keep a hold on everyone this time."

Rand snorted. "Mayhap Gerred'll hand out sweet buns, kiss us each atop our foreheads, and nurse us each to sleep upon his ample bosom." He pushed a carrot-colored strand of hair away from his eyes. "But I'll not be closing my eyes while he's around."

"You know . . ." Bacchus lowered his voice below his usual bellow. "When Clevon took over the Guild, he was about the same age we are now."

They'd all been thinking the same thing, but leave it to Bacchus to voice it. James scanned his peripheral vision to see if anybody could overhear them. By his companions' silence, he could tell they were doing the same. Thankfully, the minstrel's singing kept their voices from traveling far. "I've no interest in being guildleader," he finally said. "It's like fighting to rule a privy. Ending up on top just puts you first to be pissed on."

Bacchus roared in approval. "But the wallhuggers piss gold. Comes in helpful, even if it stinks." The city's noblemen, called such because they lived so close to the Palace wall, had recently begun to notice the Guild's potential usefulness. More than one of the Guild's senior men were in the noblemen's pockets.

Rand cleared his throat. "We can argue all night about whether the headship is worth the fight, but we might not have a choice. Especially you." He jerked his head in James's direction. "You think Gerred'll just take you at your word, that you'll be a good obedient lad?"

Bacchus nodded in slow agreement, and James didn't contradict them. He'd long been at odds with Gerred.

"There's one more thing the lass overheard," said James. "She also said that someone will flip my quarters tomorrow while me and Bacchus run the job."

"Really?" The scowl dropped from Rand's face. "We can check that, at least."

"You working tomorrow?" asked James.

Rand downed the rest of his ale. "I am now."

Chapter Two

JAMES HAD BEEN fifteen and covered in blood when he first met Clevon. A bar fight had gotten out of hand, and James had hidden in a nearby alleyway to avoid the Red Shields. But it wasn't Palace soldiers who discovered him. Instead, a plainly dressed man with a sun-darkened face and unshaven chin had come into the alley.

"None of that blood is your own, is it, lad?" Clevon had asked.

James didn't answer. The drunkard from the fight wasn't his first kill—James had learned early on to strike first and strike hard—but the aftermath still wasn't easy. He didn't like the feel of someone else's blood drying on his skin.

Clevon continued. "You're fast, and you don't hesitate. You were clear across the room by the time anyone even noticed the fool had been stuck." Clevon reached into his belt pouch and pulled out James's knife. "This your only knife?"

Leaving it in the man's body had been beyond foolish. James gathered himself to fight.

"Never carry just one knife," said Clevon. He studied the blade, rotating it so that it reflected light onto the alley walls. "But I'll make you a deal. I give your knife back and hide you from the Red Shields—if you come work for me."

That was how James had joined the Guild. Bacchus and Rand had come in around the same time. The rest of their cohort had either dropped out or died since then, but James found that the work suited him. He was good at it, and over the years he grew used to the feel of blood on his hands.

The job today was a routine one, which meant that James and Bacchus wouldn't know the specifics until they spoke to Gerred. The Guild's second-in-command held court in various locations—sometimes public, sometimes private. Today, he was in the back room of a carpenter's shop.

The smell of sawdust and the soft crunch of wood shavings underfoot greeted them as they entered a room cluttered with tools and lumber. Gerred sat at the carpenter's work table and acknowledged them with a nod. He was middle-aged, with a paunch that testified to his recent success, though anyone who mistook his girth for weakness did so at his own risk. A few of Gerred's subordinates were scattered by the walls, and behind Gerred stood a man who was fast becoming familiar to James. The man wore the clothes of a commoner, but his bearing gave him away. He stood tall and looked at people as if they existed at his pleasure. It was Lord Hamel, one of the richest noblemen in Forge. He'd always believed in spreading his influence, and he didn't restrict himself to legal means. Not for the first time, James wondered how much of his bread and butter came from Hamel's coffers.

"We're errand boys for the wallhuggers," Bacchus muttered. For once, he had the good sense to keep his voice low.

James didn't give any indication of hearing him, though he agreed. Talesinger accounts of the age-old Assassins Guild abounded with romance and mystique, but actually, the Guild's current incarnation was pale ash compared to what it once was. A hundred years ago, Guild members had been feared and influential. Nowadays, they were just hired thugs who did unpleasant jobs for pay. James's own jobs had become more menial over the past few years, though he suspected this had more to do with Gerred taking over job assignments than with the wallhuggers' meddlings.

"Ho, Gerred," James said. "How are things?"

Gerred had been writing in a ledger and put his pen down. James did have to give the man credit for being organized. Gerred's meticulousness had brought a new efficiency to Guild operations. "We've got trouble with Red Shields coming after our men," said Gerred.

"Is that so?" James let the question fall with an unfinished note.

Gerred gave them a probing look. "Clevon's dead," he said abruptly.

James briefly considered feigning surprise but decided against it. Gerred needed to know that he wasn't able to hide as much as he wished.

"When'd you plan on telling us?" asked Bacchus.

"I told you just now, din't I?"

There was a shifting of energy within the room, and James felt eyes settle on him, waiting for his next move. If the others were expecting a show, they'd be disappointed. James kept his expression carefully neutral. "When?" asked James.

"Six days ago. Red Shields. Three of them."

"That's unfortunate," he said.

Gerred rubbed his knuckles and squinted at them. "Things'll be shaky for a while. Can I count on your loyalty?"

"Of course," said James coolly. Around him, the other assassins settled, and the tension dissipated a notch.

Again, a long stare from Gerred. Then, he cleared his throat. "The job today is for Lord Hamel. An associate owes him money." He handed them a name and address on a parchment. James took it, since Bacchus couldn't read. James himself had only learned to do so after he'd noticed all the leaders in the Guild were literate.

Gerred gestured toward the parchment. "You know him, don't you?"

"Name looks familiar. He still hasn't paid up?"

Behind Gerred, Lord Hamel cleared his throat. "He's owed me money for several weeks now." The nobleman spoke with an elegant diction. "Be more persuasive this time, will you? I don't imagine that will be a problem for the two of you."

Bacchus snorted. "It won't."

They took their leave. Most of the city had gone to sleep, and the streets were quiet. After they had gone a few blocks, Rand materialized from the shadows and fell in step with them. "Any news?" he asked.

"Clevon's dead," said Bacchus. "Gerred 'fessed up."

Rand cursed under his breath. "Think Gerred'll take over?"

"Seems he already has," said James.

Their conversation fell off as they reached the man's house. James nodded, and the three of them moved in.

The door was in such disrepair that it swung open with a single kick from Bacchus. James watched as the other two dragged a disoriented man out of bed. Their victim was still blinking and shaking his head when they dumped him in front of James. Rand pulled him to his feet and held him firmly by the arms.

"One hundred coppers, due three months ago," said James. "You remember, don't you?"

As the man came to his senses, he started to gibber about his health. James exchanged a glance with Bacchus, who rolled up his sleeves and moved closer with a grin. Bacchus enjoyed this type of work.

James watched him deliver the first few blows. Beatings had to be done, but he didn't take pleasure in them. After a while, he caught Rand's eye. The redheaded man nodded. He would keep Bacchus in line, and James was free to go home and check on the dancing girl's other warning.

James lived in a single room with a sloping ceiling, tucked above a smithy. Its location meant that he got some extra heat in the winter from the forge below, though it was sweltering in the summer, and the blacksmith's hammer constantly echoed through the walls. The noise was a boon tonight, since it hid sounds of his return. He climbed the stairs quietly and timed the turn of his key to a hammer stroke. Then he threw the door open.

A man was by his bed, sliding his hand under the mattress. In the moment the intruder stared dumbfounded, James closed the distance between them, dodging the man's hasty punch. James threw a solid blow to his stomach, and when the man doubled over, brought the hilt of his dagger down over his head. The intruder crumpled to the ground, stunned. James checked him for weapons. He found three daggers— one at his waist and two on his shins, which James tossed into the corner. The man stirred, and James ground his knee into his throat.

"Who sent you?" He kept his voice soft, speaking between the rings of the blacksmith's hammer. "Don't lie to me."

The man hesitated, eyes rolling in confusion. James repeated the question, opening two slashes on the man's cheek for emphasis.

"Gerred." The man's voice was tinged with panic.

Somehow, James wasn't surprised. "What did he want?" he asked.

Another hesitation, which disappeared when James moved the knife closer. "I was to look for letters, money. Anything to see if you were gathering folk to you, with Clevon gone."

James flicked his knife across the man's throat, just hard enough to draw blood. The man cursed at him, and James dragged him to his feet.

"Let's go pay Gerred a visit."

*   *   *

To some extent, the bad blood between James and Gerred was Bacchus's fault. Bacchus had been just as reckless with his insults during his early years as he was now. One day, a few years after Bacchus had joined the Guild, an older assassin named Nathaniel lost his temper and took a swing at him. But there was a reason Bacchus could afford to be so freely offensive. Within moments, the younger assassin had Nathaniel pinned against a table, a manic grin on his face as he tightened his grip on the older man's throat. Other Guild members broke in between the two fighters before any blood was shed.

It should have ended like that, with bruised pride and nothing else. But a few days later, James overheard Nathaniel making plans to ambush Bacchus. James had watched the first fight without interfering—he'd had no special love for Bacchus back then, thinking him unpredictable and dangerous. But James disliked Nathaniel even more than he disliked Bacchus. The older assassin was part of Gerred's inner circle and all too willing to abuse his position. It was why Nathaniel had even dared plan the ambush—infighting within the Guild was against Clevon's rules, but Nathaniel thought himself untouchable.

Nathaniel's crew was successful in their ambush. They had Bacchus on his knees, spitting blood, when James intervened. As it was, they didn't see James until two men were already down with their throats slit. James would have preferred not to kill them—it meant more trouble from Clevon later on— but he couldn't have gone up against four if he'd held back.

When Gerred found out, he demanded that Clevon execute James. Instead, Clevon pardoned him. Gerred and James maintained an uneasy truce after that. With the old guildleader gone though, it seemed that Gerred was taking more direct steps.

The carpenter's shop had emptied considerably by the time James dragged the bound and gagged spy through the door. The only people left were Gerred, Lord Hamel, and two men that James recognized as Hamel's bodyguards. Gerred stopped talking when James entered. His gaze went first to James, then to his prisoner, lingering in particular on the cut across the man's neck.

"Please excuse me," Gerred said to Lord Hamel.

There was a touch of a smirk on Hamel's lips as he led his guards past James and his prisoner. James got the impression that the nobleman was amused by the hint of internal trouble. As the door closed behind Hamel, James turned back to Gerred.

"I brought him back this time," said James. "Next time, I won't."

Gerred sat back in his chair, showing no more remorse than if James had accused him of forgetting his birthday. "I needed to know the loyalty of my men, with Clevon gone."

At least he hadn't tried to deny it. "Next time you're wondering about my loyalties, ask me."

"You know that's not good enough. If you had nothing to hide, you had nothing to worry about. If you did . . " Gerred shrugged.

James dumped the spy onto the ground. A small cloud of sawdust rose up off the floor. "I won't follow a guildleader who thinks he can sift through my quarters on a whim."

Gerred's eyes narrowed. "Careful, James. Do you realize what you're saying?"

James stopped himself. He hadn't meant to overtly threaten defection. "I'm willing to work under you, Gerred. If you treat me fairly, I won't cause trouble. But I won't stand for spies."

Gerred glanced at the candle on his desk. It hadn't yet burned half its length. "You were hardly gone an hour. Rather impressive, to finish a job and make it back so soon."

"I work quickly." James couldn't quite dredge up the motivation for a more convincing lie.

"I'll wager you did," grunted Gerred, taking one last look at the candle. "You're a good assassin, James, provided you do as you're told. Finish the jobs you're given, follow instructions. You've been running jobs with Rand and Bacchus for a while now. I think it's time you pair up with some others. I wouldn't want you getting stale, working with the same crew all the time."

And of course, separating him from Rand and Bacchus would make it harder for them to cause Gerred trouble. The guildleader was watching James carefully now, seeing if he'd provoked a response. Briefly, James entertained the thought of drawing his blade. Gerred was good, but he'd slowed with age. In a fair fight, the odds would be on James's side, but Hamel and his bodyguards were just outside. Somehow, James suspected that starting a fight was exactly what the guildleader wanted him to do.

He kept his expression carefully neutral. "Very well then. If that's what you think is best."

Chapter Three

BACCHUS SLAMMED HIS mug down on the table. "Now he wants to split us up? He'll pair us with his lapdogs, mark my words. We won't be able to do anything without him knowing again." They were back at the Scorned Maiden, discussing the previous night's events.

Rand nodded in agreement. "Gerred's tightening his grip."

James didn't reply. They were right, and he had nothing more to add. Instead, he looked across the room to where the auburn-haired dancing girl was performing. The girl's onstage persona was completely different from the way she'd presented herself two nights ago. When she danced, she was striking—animated, unreserved, and alluring. When the girl had approached two nights ago, though, she'd gone out of the way not to draw attention to herself.

Bacchus followed James's gaze and whistled appreciatively. "You talk to her yet?" he asked James.

James shook his head. "Later."

"Why don't you stop ogling her and think about how we're going to live out the next month?" said Rand. A serving girl came to ask if they wanted more ale, and Rand shot her a glance that sent her scurrying away.

James let out a breath and turned back to Rand. He pressed his ankle against the side of his boot, and the knife he kept there pushed comfortingly back. "What are our options then?"

Bacchus cracked his knuckles. "I say the bastard's lived out his time on top. Clevon was no genius, but he was honest with us, at least. Gerred'll stab anyone in the back if it means more gold for him."

"If either of you wants to fight for the top, go ahead. I've no interest in it," said James. "We've been here ten years. We know how it works by now. Clevon lived a comfortable life, and Gerred still does. We all joined thinking someday we'd live like them. Only now we know how many rank and file want the same thing, and how many bodies we'd have to crawl over to get there."

"We could outfight anyone in the Guild," said Bacchus. The eagerness in his voice was hard to miss.

James shrugged. "Mayhap we could, but all it takes is one knife in the back. And all this for what? So we can be finished off by a Red Shield in ten years?"

Rand cleared his throat. "You're forgetting that Gerred in't exactly giving us a choice in the matter. It doesn't matter whether we're loyal to him or not. He's already convinced you'll fight to be head, and your conversation last night didn't calm his fears, I'll guarantee you that."

While Bacchus's thoughts were always written clear on his face, James had always found Rand harder to read. He was somewhat of a puzzle: closed-mouthed about his past and effective enough at his job, but he clearly didn't love it like Bacchus did. And though they'd saved each other's lives dozens of times, James realized he didn't know what Rand really felt about the headship, or the Guild for that matter.

"You're right, Rand. Gerred'll likely not give us a choice about the issue—if we stick around in Forge," said James. "But none of us has ties to the city. What's stopping us from leaving altogether?"

Bacchus gave James a sidelong glance, comprehension dawning on his face. Rand looked impressed as well. As his companions chewed over his words, James's gaze wandered back to the dancing girl. She'd put bells on her ankles and wrists now and shook them in time to the music. Light from the hearth, the table lamps, and the candle chandeliers played off her movements and gave her skin a reddish hue. A few times, he thought she looked in his direction.

"Not a bad idea," Rand finally said. "I've always wanted to see Parna."

"Set up there?" asked Bacchus.

"Or just travel for a while," said James.

"We in't got the coin," said Rand, his scowl creeping back. "We'd need supplies, horses, better traveling clothes than we've got if we want to survive the winter."

He was right. The forest roads were not friendly to travelers, and Parna would present its own set of obstacles once they got there.

Bacchus drained his flagon and slammed it down on the table, his signal that he was done talking for the night. "Too much worrying and too little ale. We can decide tomorrow."

The music had stopped. James glanced around and saw that the dancing girl stood near the back of the dining room. Again, she'd changed out of her costume and into her homespun dress.

"Fine. We think about it," he said, pushing back from the table.

Bacchus grinned when he saw where James was looking. "Don't be up too late," he said as James walked away.

The girl straightened as James approached. She looked him calmly in the eye, though she fidgeted with her fingers as if grasping and ungrasping an invisible ball.

"You were right," he said.

Relief flickered across her face. Her expression was guarded, and she stood in such a way as to emphasize the empty space between them. James didn't see even a hint of the coquettishness he'd seen from her onstage. "You caught someone then?" she asked.

He moved closer and lowered his voice. "How did you come to be so good at overhearing Guild secrets?"

He'd half expected her to put more distance between them, but she stood her ground. "I'm quiet. Men don't notice me."

"I doubt that."

He had the satisfaction of seeing a flush rise in her cheeks. "Perhaps," she said. "But they forget I have ears." When he didn't reply, she spoke again. "What now?"

"I owe you my thanks. I'll hear you out."

She glanced around the room, and her gaze settled on a group of men close enough to overhear them.

"Mayhap we can take a walk?" he asked, catching her meaning.

They headed to the door. She looked surprised when he held it open for her. James gave her a sardonic smile and waved her out. The air was brisk, just chilly enough to bring a cloak to mind.

"What's your name?" he asked.

"Thalia."

They walked down a ways, past the busier streets until no one was in sight. The roads were narrow and the night was dark. The upper floors of houses on each side jutted out overhead to block the moonlight. Nevertheless, Thalia followed him without hesitation, as if they were old friends instead of a maid and an assassin.

"You're brave. Or very trusting," he told her.

"Just determined." Her shoulders were hunched as she walked, her jaw set.

"And what are you determined for?"

19

The sound from the crowds they'd left faded away completely, and the streets were quiet. They slowed to a stop at the mouth of a narrow alleyway. Thalia clutched her elbows and faced him, angling her head up to look him in the eye.

"There's a man. I want him dead."

She'd said as much earlier. "Who?" he asked.

"A wallhugger."

James laughed. The girl was either stupid or suicidal. "Not just enough to hire an assassin, is it? You want to kill a nobleman."

She didn't react to his derision. "Will you do it?"

He shook his head. "Too dangerous."

"They're men like anyone else."

"Men with money and power, and scores of Red Shields at their beck and call. Folk who value their lives don't meddle in wallhugger affairs. I owe you for your help, but this is too much."

As he turned away, she called after him. "Wait!" For the first time, a hint of desperation crept into her voice. "If you won't kill him for me, at least help me."

So the girl wasn't quite as cool and calm as she'd appeared. "How?" he asked.

Thalia swallowed. She was trying to compose herself again, with only partial success. "Show me how to kill him myself."

"You?" He looked from her eyes to the rest of her body, making no effort to hide his disdain at her fragile limbs. He took her wrist in his hand, holding his hand up to show her where his fingers overlapped. He wasn't gentle, and her eyes teared up, though she didn't pull away.

"How strong do you need to be, really, to push a dagger home?" she whispered. "He's not very powerful. Just a minor nobleman. And I don't look like a killer. He won't be expecting it from me." There was an intensity in her eyes, either ambition or despair, he couldn't tell.

"I can offer you more than a simple payment," she continued. "I have connections with trade caravans. You must need money, with your guildleader gone. I can give you access to rare goods. Expensive ones. You could gain much by doing business with the traders."

He raised an eyebrow. "Are you suggesting I branch out into honest trade?"

"It's not . . . entirely honest." She spoke carefully. "But it could be lucrative. One run with them could earn you enough to outfit you comfortably for travel. And being friends with the caravans never hurts if you're planning to take to the road."

James wasn't sure if he completely hid his surprise at her words. Apparently, he was no more alert to her eavesdropping than Gerred's men. But he did need money, and if she really could deliver what she promised . . . "Are you lying to me?" he asked.

"I promise you I'm not. Give me a few weeks. See what I have to offer, and what you can teach me. Then you can be done with me."

*   *   *

She came cautiously through the door the next afternoon, taking in his sparse room—the bed, his trunk, the window— with a few quick glances. When the blacksmith started hammering downstairs, her brow furrowed with annoyance, but she said nothing.

"You live here?" she asked.

"It in't the Palace, but it's got walls."

"I grew up in a covered wagon. At least this doesn't blow over in a storm."

She moved as if to sit on the bed but thought better of it and crouched by the wall. James sat in the space she had just avoided and studied her. She sat with her dress bunched around her, and her hair fanned over her shoulders. Though her face was carefully blank, her fingers tapped restlessly against her knees.

"You're serious about this?" said James. "You want to kill a nobleman."

She nodded, studying the wall behind him as if there were an image there only she could see.

"And you want this enough to put your life in danger? Why come to me?"

She was silent for a moment, pulling at the hem of her dress. "I've been watching you," she said slowly. "You think before you act. You don't get carried away by your drink like your friend Bacchus. You look at the serving girls, but you don't grab them. And I know you're good at what you do."

He raised an eyebrow. "You do?"

"Three months ago. When the fight broke out in the Scorned Maiden."

He vaguely remembered that fight. A merchant and his friends had taken offense to one of Bacchus's cracks, and James had come to his defense. "I didn't kill anyone in that fight," he said. It was better not to, if he wanted to continue to frequent the tavern.

"But you could have. I've seen my share of brawls. I know a good fighter from a bad one." She spoke with the objective tone of a seamstress picking thread.

"So who is this mysterious nobleman?"

Her expression became guarded. "You're not killing him for me. Just showing me how to use a knife."

He'd thought her reckless, with the way she'd followed him into the alley last night. But perhaps he'd underestimated her. "How long have you wanted him dead?"

"Two years."

"Did something happen two years ago?"

"Yes." She didn't volunteer any more information.

He shrugged. "Keep your secrets for now. One wallhugger's the same as another to me. But if you really want me to teach you right, you've eventually got to tell me more. I'll need to know how close you can get to him. If he's guarded, and how well. If he's trained with weapons. But right now, I want to know more about your connection with the caravans."

She relaxed a bit at this new line of questioning. "I grew up with the trade caravans and traveled with them until a few years ago," she said. "As you know, the Palace puts limits on what can be sold. It reserves some rare goods for itself by making it illegal to sell them to others in the city. I have friends though, who could be persuaded to overlook those laws."

There was a knock at the door, and Thalia snapped her head to the sound. "That's Rand and Bacchus," said James. "Will you tell them the same thing you just told me?"

"Do you trust them?"

"With my life."

She thought for a moment, then nodded.

Bacchus winked at Thalia as he came in, and Rand nodded curtly in her direction. She ignored Bacchus and returned Rand's nod as James filled them in.

"What kind of rare goods?" asked Bacchus when James finished.

"Spices. Tapestries," said Thalia.

"And what would we need to do? How long to set everything up?" asked James.

"You'd have to meet them outside the city and smuggle the goods past the city gates. After that, it's up to you. You could have a run set up in three weeks."

23

"Sounds like a lot of work," said Rand. He trailed off and gave Thalia a sideways glance.

Thalia gathered her skirts. "I can leave, if you'd like to talk things over."

"Come back tomorrow," said James. With the girl's knack for picking up information, kicking her out now probably wouldn't accomplish much. But they might as well keep the illusion of secrecy.

He waited until she stepped out to the street below before he turned back to Bacchus and Rand. "What do you think?"

"We'd need buyers," said Rand.

"For spices, it'd be rich merchants or noblemen. But they'd definitely buy," said James.

Rand bobbed his head in acknowledgment of James's reasoning. "Three weeks to get the goods, another few days after that to wrap things up. Gerred'll be suspicious if he sees us doing anything unusual. "

"We keep it from Gerred," said James. "He'd just assume the worst. Better if he doesn't know our plans until we're gone. If we play nice, I don't think he'll do anything rash in the meantime. He's too careful for that."

Bacchus straightened with a slap of his thigh. "Let's do it. But we keep our options open. Maybe we'll decide the privy's worth going for after all."

James gave a tight smile. "It's always good to have options."

*   *   *

He handed her a stiletto the length of her hand and molded her fingers around the handle. Her hands were slender and her nails were delicately rounded, though her palms were calloused. The two of them stood in the cramped space between his bed and the window, holding the blade between them.

"You can wear this dagger under your sleeves. Then, when you get your chance . . ." James guided the knife toward his own throat. "Go for the neck—the blood vessels and the windpipe. You'll have to be close for that. Quick."

He lowered the stiletto until its tip grazed his neck just above his collarbone. Her eyes widened, and she looked to his face.

He smiled and tightened his hands around her wrist. "Never let your guard down. Never trust anyone, and never leave yourself vulnerable."

"What if I'd surprised you just now? I could have been sent by someone to kill you."

"You wouldn't have."

She arched her eyebrow. "I wouldn't have killed you?"

"You wouldn't have surprised me." He continued. "You have to be aware. If someone is this close to you, holding a weapon, you need to be on your guard. I'm watching your eyes, your shoulders. I'm aware of how you're standing, where your balance is. If you tighten your muscles to strike, I'll feel it in your arm. You should be doing the same with me."

Her eyes were cautious as she took in what he said. And he watched her look down, taking in his arms, the angle of his chest. Her gaze went inward and her lips fell slightly open as she tried to get a feel for his balance. Standing as close as they were, he could smell a light perfume on her skin.

Thalia seemed to remember herself. She disengaged her wrist and backed away.

"What makes a lass like you into a killer?" he asked.

She shot him an annoyed look, and the tension left the room. "I didn't hire you to delve into my past."

"Are you sure you want to do this? It changes you, you know, your first kill."

A smile touched her lips, a hint of a challenge. "You're quite determined to have me think this over. Do you regret *your* first kill?"

It was an interesting question, and he gave it some thought. "No," he finally said. "I regret not having done it sooner."

"Who was it?" She tilted her head in anticipation of a tale. "Some Red Shield?"

"My father." He smiled when her eyes widened. "I'll make you a deal. You can keep your secrets, and I'll keep mine."

"Fair enough." In another moment, she was all business again. "So if I want to cut his throat, I have to get in close to him."

"It's the only way. You can't beat him in a fair fight."

She turned away. "I know I'm not as strong as a man."

He shrugged. "And you never will be. But I killed grown men before I came of age. If you can't rely on strength, you rely on stealth. Surprise is your strongest asset, so make sure the first time kills." He paused. "If you kill him while he's alone, you might be able to escape. If there are others with him, you won't. Either way, you're just as likely to die from this venture as your mark. You know that, right?"

"I do."

Her voice was level, but he thought he caught a flash of despair in her eyes. What secrets was she holding that would drive her to do this? But that was her business.

Thalia sheathed the blade and laid it across the palm of her hand, feeling its weight. "What about poison?" she asked.

"Poison? What of it?"

"Then I could make sure I kill him the first time."

He waved her suggestion away and turned toward the window. "You've been listening to too many talesingers. Poisons are a thing of the past." On the street below, a raven-haired boy pushed a cart of fruit. Strange to think that most folk might go their whole lives without plotting someone's death. When James turned back to Thalia, she was gazing calmly up at him.

"Why?" she asked.

"Poison is cheating. A blade is all you need."

His dismissal had no visible effect on her. "Do you really think it's cheating, or is it because you don't have the means? The Guild isn't exactly what it used to be."

She was more right than he wanted to admit. A hundred years ago, when the Guild's influence had ranged from the slums to the Palace, assassins had used poisons to great effect. There had still been talk of venoms during James's early days at the Guild. The older assassins had told stories— exaggerated, no doubt, but detailed enough to ring true. These days, they barely had the coin to keep their crew fed, let alone maintain the funds and connections to acquire exotic substances. James felt a surge of irritation. "Do you want my help or not? You can pursue your poisons if that's what you wish. But don't bother me about it."

"What if I were to tell you that I know a trader who sells lizard skin venom?"

He froze. "You lie."

"It would cost you of course. But it's there."

James wondered when the girl would stop surprising him. "Lizard skin is a blade poison. You'd still need to draw blood. If you were in the Guild, I'd tell you not to use it lest your knife skills grow weak. But in your case, it could be useful."

Chapter Four

THALIA ARRANGED FOR James to be introduced to the caravaners at their campsite. James met her at the city gates so Thalia could show him the way. Her hair was pulled back in a scarf, and she'd traded her dress for rugged trousers that accentuated the lines of her legs. Thalia traveled the forest paths with the same grace she lent to her dancing.

"These friends of yours. How well do you know them?" asked James.

"They're not my home caravan, but I've known Alvie since I was small enough to sit on his knee. He's trustworthy."

They broke through a clearing where seven covered wagons were circled around a firepit. A handful of men and women went about their business, weaving between the wagons and occasionally ducking into them. James had seen caravaners before when they traded in the city, but he'd had little interaction with them. They were a close-knit bunch and mostly kept to themselves, though James had heard that they were protective and fiercely loyal, both to their own caravans and to others that they formed alliances with.

"How often are they here?" asked James.

"Once a fortnight, perhaps," said Thalia.

The back flap of a wagon opened, and a bald, stocky man stepped out. He had a face resembling a walrus, with a curled mustache in place of tusks. "Thalia!" he said.

Thalia responded with the first genuine smile James had seen from her.

Alvie pulled the dancing girl into an embrace. "Still here then, on your mad quest?"

"Until it's done." She spoke quietly, but something about her tone suggested that she was holding her ground in a long disagreement between the two of them.

Alvie's expression became more guarded when he saw James. "You're the buyer?"

"I can get your goods past the Red Shield checkpoints," said James.

"You're not afraid of the Palace?" The trader looked him up and down.

James smiled. "More marks against me won't make a difference. But why would *you* take this risk?"

Alvie gestured in the direction of the city. "The Palace keeps our prices low by prohibiting us from selling to others. I travel far for those goods. I want to make my fair due."

"I assume Thalia's told you that we're only planning one run. We don't plan to be in Forge much longer."

"Plenty of money in one run," said Alvie. "And if things go well, there's no reason we couldn't continue this elsewhere."

"Fair enough," said James. "We'll need to find buyers, but I'd like to see the wares first."

"Certainly." Alvie gestured to Thalia. "It's in the fifth wagon."

As Thalia disappeared behind the wagon, Alvie turned his eye toward James. "You know her well?"

"No. She sought me out."

Alvie looked him over again. James suspected that this time Alvie wasn't evaluating his abilities as a smuggler. He wasn't sure what the caravaner could discern from his appearance, but whatever Alvie saw didn't clear the suspicion from his eyes. "I'd ask your help in keeping her out of trouble, but I suppose that's not your arrangement with her."

James smiled, not missing the layers of questions behind the caravaner's remark. "She's not looking to stay out of trouble." If Alvie wanted to know more about their arrangement, he'd have to get it out of Thalia.

"Are you involved with her?" Alvie asked bluntly.

"Why do you want to know?"

"We both stand to lose much if this venture goes wrong. Thalia says you're trustworthy, but I need to know if anything's clouding her judgment."

James didn't believe for a moment that the man's concern was for business reasons. Not with the protective way he watched over the girl. James supposed there was no point in needlessly antagonizing the man. "She keeps her distance," he said.

Alvie gave a quick nod, apparently satisfied, and looked to where Thalia was climbing out of the wagon. "She's changed," he said. "Since she lost her sister."

The caravaner was watching him for a reaction. James gave a noncommittal shrug. "I just do what she pays me to do."

There was a twitch of frustration in Alvie's expression. He might have said more, but Thalia was already coming back with a large box. If she suspected she'd been the topic of conversation, she gave no sign of it. Alvie placed the box on the back of the nearest wagon and opened it. The smell of a half dozen spices filled the air.

"Cinnamon, saffron, curries from Minadel," said Alvie. "I can give you some samples to show to your buyers."

"That will work. I should have buyers ready in a fortnight."

Thalia stood on her toes and kissed Alvie lightly on the cheek. "You'll bring me the venom next time?" When Alvie stayed silent, she added, "If you don't, I'll just go forward without it."

For a moment, it looked like Alvie was going to argue, but he gave a defeated nod and squeezed her tight. "Take care of yourself."

*   *   *

Thalia danced again that night. Every time James watched her, he noticed something new. This time, it was the way she arched her neck when she bent to the music. It was a small detail, sensual and carefree at once.

"You bed her yet?" asked Bacchus. "If you're not interested, I want a try."

"Stay away from her," he said, eyes fixed on the dance. Actually, James wasn't sure why he hadn't tried anything yet. He'd never been shy of women, and there were always some adventurous serving girls eager to roll with an assassin. But Thalia had made it clear from the beginning that their arrangement was purely business—going out of her way to wipe off her eye paint and rouge before she came to talk to him, refusing to sit on his bed. This was limited only to her off stage dealings. When Thalia was on stage, she was enchanting—all swaying hips and fluttering lashes.

Presently, the music stopped, and she came by their table. Her cheeks were flushed from the exercise, and the hair around her face was damp with sweat. She'd been in good spirits after visiting the caravan.

Thalia made a barely perceptible gesture toward a table in the corner.

"Over there. That's your guildleader, isn't it?"

James glanced over. "That's Gerred."

"And who's that with him?"

"One of the noblemen he caters to. Goes by Steffen."

Thalia shifted herself carefully so no one but James could see her lips. "And his real name, is it Hamel?"

He really needed to stop being surprised when the girl knew something she shouldn't. James gave a discrete nod.

Her face took on a focus that he'd never seen before. "I need to speak with him."

"Why?"

She hesitated a split second. "He has connections."

Why was the girl flat-out set on diving into the messiest circumstances possible? "He's dangerous," he said.

"Please. Introduce me. Let me dance for them," she said. Again, there was something in her eyes. The same fiery desperation that had been there when she'd first asked him for help. It bothered James how little he knew about her, but he was curious about her request, and perhaps it would be a good idea to stay close to Gerred.

"Just this once," he said, standing up from his chair. He wasn't sure whether the flash of triumph across her face bode well or ill.

Gerred looked to be in the middle of a long speech, leaning across the table toward Hamel as the nobleman listened with a half-interested expression. The guildleader shot James a look that was anything but welcoming. James pretended not to notice.

"Can I join you?" James pulled up a chair, knowing that Gerred wouldn't turn him away once he was there, lest he give Hamel an impression that he didn't have full control over his crew. But the look Gerred turned on him when he sat down was even more hostile than James had expected. Belatedly, he realized that what might have once simply been an impudent gesture from a young upstart was now being interpreted as an attempt from a rival to poach Gerred's allies. Well, it was too late to back out now, and part of him enjoyed seeing Gerred off balance.

James turned to Lord Hamel. "Good to see you. Steffen, is it?"

Lord Hamel nodded amiably, though the spark in his eyes suggested that the nobleman was well aware of everything that had passed between the two assassins. Once again, James reminded himself not to underestimate this wallhugger.

"What brings you to the city today?" James asked.

"Just discussing some plans with Gerred." Hamel did a respectable job of hiding his high-class diction, though he couldn't quite lose his air of command. But then, perhaps he didn't want to blend in too completely with the masses.

James nodded gravely. "There are always things to get done. Gerred's the right man for the job, though. He's done much to strengthen our Guild's workings." James had the satisfaction of seeing Gerred's brow furrow slightly in confusion.

"I'm glad to hear it. It is said that the best measure of a man lies in the opinions of those he commands," said Hamel.

"Wisely said," said James, without a hint of mockery. "Tell me, Steffen. Have you been to the Scorned Maiden before?"

"Not for many years." Hamel surveyed the surroundings in a way that made James aware of the ill-fitted window shutters and rotting ceiling beams. The smell of sweat and ale was strong tonight. "It has its charms."

James took a long draught from his drink. "The ale is middling, but the dancers are some of the best in the city." He raised a hand to Thalia. "A dance, to entertain my friend here." He flipped a coin to the lute player in the corner.

Thalia danced well. James had never seen her so given to a performance, and she only had eyes for Hamel. The nobleman watched with an appreciative eye, and after a while James itched to cut that leer off his face. But Thalia was encouraging him, tossing her auburn hair and swaying her hips. Gerred scowled as well, shooting suspicious looks at James every so often. But seeing how pleased Hamel was, Gerred didn't complain.

When the dance was over, Hamel waved Thalia over. She approached them boldly, her eyes sparkling with promises.

"What is your name?"

"Thalia."

"Beautiful, Thalia. Truly beautiful." Lord Hamel pulled up a chair for her, and Thalia joined them at the table.

Chapter Five

THALIA WAS NOTICEABLY tired when she came to James's quarters the next afternoon. Paler, if it was even possible, with circles under her eyes.

"Didn't sleep well last night?" James asked. He didn't bother toning down his sarcasm.

"I don't want to talk about it." There was a brokenness to her tone that might have stopped him under different circumstances, but he wasn't feeling charitable. All he could see was Thalia under Hamel's arm, smiling and laughing as the nobleman pulled her even closer. Hamel's lips against her hair as he whispered in her ear. And to add insult to injury, she was now back in her homespun gown with her makeup removed, playing the innocent.

"I didn't think you had it in you," he said.

She didn't say anything, just turned away from him so that her hair hid her face from view. James's anger boiled over. He grabbed her wrist. Too forcefully, and she gasped.

"Did you go to his bed?"

"What is it to you?" she said.

Part of him had still hoped she'd deny it. James's lips curled in disgust. "You really are dedicated, aren't you? If you're planning to use Hamel to reach your mark, you're playing with fire. One wrong step with him—"

It seemed that something snapped in her, because her timidity fell away. Thalia whipped her head up, eyes ablaze. "Don't be blind, James. Look at me. Do you think I enjoyed it?"

They were almost nose to nose, and her voice was threatening to crack. It was enough to make him pause. He pulled back and took in the hollow hopelessness of her face, the pallor of her skin. She watched him, eyes wide. Then Thalia seemed to gather herself. She stood up on her toes, eyes half lidded, and touched her lips to his. He knew she was just trying to distract him, to give him what she thought he desired. For a long moment, he stood unmoving against the pressure of her lips, but finally he tilted his face ever so slightly to meet hers.

This was the signal she was waiting for. Thalia pressed into him, urgent now, and a rush of heat filled James. Her lips were soft, her breath warm. He'd known he wanted her, but hadn't realized how much. Thalia's body was strong but pliant, just as he'd imagined, her restless fingers finding purchase in his arms and his shoulders. He buried his fingers in her hair, his frustration adding a savagery to his movements as he bore her toward his bed, sliding his hands down her back to pull at the lacing of her gown.

Only to see, in his mind's eye, Hamel doing the same thing hours earlier.

He pushed her away. She gasped and fell onto the bed.

"What are you doing?" His voice was hoarse, and he struggled to catch his breath.

Slowly, she came to her senses. Her cheeks were flushed, her eyes uncertain. "I don't know," she whispered. "I'm sorry."

He stepped away from her, putting space between them. "No more secrets, Thalia. What are you really trying to do?"

36

She opened her mouth, but no sound came out. For a long time, she stood there, caught between speaking and silence.

"Hamel is my mark," she finally said. She watched him, her back straight, bracing herself for his reaction.

"Hamel?" For a moment, that was all that came out of his mouth. "You're mad," he finally said. "You told me that your mark was *not* very powerful."

Her chin lifted slightly. "You wouldn't have helped me otherwise."

"You're right. I wouldn't have. He's likely been trained in combat from birth. He goes nowhere without his bodyguards. Even if you get a weapon past them, even if you kill him and escape, Hamel has so many connections, even in the city. If the Red Shields don't get you, then the Guild will." He stopped, remembering where she had just come from. "Wait, did you . . ."

She deflated at his question. "His bodyguards took my dagger before they left us alone. I told them I kept it to protect myself against drunk patrons, but they're watching me now, and they'll be searching me even more carefully in the future. There's no way I can get a knife past them now." She stared past James, eyes bleak. Then she resolutely shook her head. "It doesn't matter. I've come this far. I'll find another way. I have to."

* * *

If Rand or Bacchus noticed that James and Thalia avoided talking that night, neither of them mentioned it. His two friends spent the evening pricing Minadan spices while James looked on. Thankfully, Hamel was nowhere to be seen, but James wasn't naïve enough to think that this respite would last long.

He left the tavern early and returned to his quarters. It was quiet—no noise from the blacksmith's family through the walls. He allowed himself to light an oil lamp so he could mend a tear in his spare tunic and had just sat down on his bed when there was a knock on the door.

It was Thalia.

After a long moment, James stepped aside. Her face was downcast as she walked in, and she sat against his wall the same way as when she'd visited him the first time. Back then, she had been trying to keep him at a distance. Tonight, the act felt more like an apology. Neither of them said anything, and James returned to his mending.

After a while, she finally spoke. "Your father. Why did you kill him?"

That hadn't been the question he'd expected. Though from the vulnerability in her eyes, he would have thought it was him questioning her rather than the other way around.

"It's no big secret," he said. "My Da didn't handle his wine well. Took out his frustrations on me and my sister. One day he hit her too hard, and I fought back."

The answer didn't seem to surprise her. "What became of your sister?"

"She died."

Thalia nodded slowly in understanding. "That's why you wish you'd killed him sooner."

James laid the tunic aside. The memory was an old one, numb like a wound calloused over. "I just make sure I don't make the same mistake again."

Thalia hooked a finger under her collar and drew out a thin gold necklace that James had never noticed before. She examined it, brows furrowed, tilting the links to the light. "I've promised myself I wouldn't hesitate. That I'd do anything."

"Why do you want to kill Hamel?" he asked.

She raised her eyes, doubt in her gaze.

"Alvie says you lost your sister. Was that Hamel's doing?"

She was silent again, no longer staring at the chain in her hands but at a spot on the floor beyond it. James waited.

"Tess was four years my senior," she finally said. There was a sad note to her voice, but a measure of relief too, as if she were delivering a long suppressed confession. "Our parents died before I learned to walk, so in many ways, she was a mother to me. She taught me to dance. . . ." Thalia trailed off with a wistful smile. "She was beautiful."

After a moment, she continued. "We grew up with the caravans, but we were fascinated by life in the cities. Tess especially. When I was old enough to travel with the caravan myself, Tess came to live at Forge. It wasn't supposed to be a long trip. She just wanted to see what it was like. She danced at the Silver Plough to pay for lodging, and I visited her when the caravan passed by."

Thalia drew a shaky breath. "Lord Hamel came often to the Silver Plough. At the time, we didn't know who he was. We knew he was rich, and we knew he liked Tess. I suppose she should have known better. She never had any interest in him, but she accepted his gifts. He started to get more possessive, demanding her time. In the meantime, Tess had become close with a young man. Hamel found out about them."

Thalia suddenly raised her eyes to James, and an edge of bitterness entered her voice. "Funny how a man's mind will work. If Tess had accepted Hamel's overtures, he probably would have tired of her in a few months. But because she chose someone over him, Hamel became obsessed. He cajoled her to leave him. Then it became threats. Tess was worried, but still, she did nothing. The caravan was far off, and she didn't want to leave her lover."

Thalia closed her eyes for a moment, her eyes moving beneath her translucent lids. "They found her dead outside The Silver Plough. Her lover's body washed up in the river a few days later."

She was still fidgeting with the necklace, weaving the chain absentmindedly between her fingertips. James stepped closer and took it between his fingers. It was made of delicate gold, with links in the shape of leaves. James could tell it was valuable, far beyond the means of a girl like her.

Thalia opened her eyes. "This was hers," Thalia said. "A family heirloom. Our father gave it to her before he died."

"It's beautiful." He held the necklace one last time to the lamplight before letting it drop. "Are you sure it was Lord Hamel who killed her?"

She nodded, her voice quivering with fury. "He boasted of it afterwards. About how he'd taught the uppity dancing girl a lesson."

"And now you want to take your revenge."

"It's all I've lived for since she died." Thalia looked to her hands, and with effort, composed herself. "I shouldn't have kept this from you. I'm sorry," she said. "But I've told you everything now. If you're still willing to help me . . ." She was pleading with him. Begging, really, her desperation naked on her face.

James turned away from her. It had been a foolish venture from the beginning. Even with the promise of trade with the caravans, the idea of training a girl to bring down a nobleman was preposterous. Thalia had misled him about her mark, and James had no way of knowing if she was lying now. But he didn't think she was lying. . . . He hoped he wouldn't regret what he was about to say.

"You can still get to Hamel," he said.

A cautious hope lit up in her eyes. "I can?"

"You say his bodyguards took your blade. Did they take anything else? Your hairpins? Jewelry?"

She shook her head.

"It's harder to deliver venom without a blade, but any sharpened object will do. I can teach you."

"Thank you." She was tentative, as if she were afraid he'd take it back.

"It won't be easy," he said.

"I know."

There wasn't much more to say after that. James finished his stitching and folded his tunic while she stayed silent, lost in her thoughts. After a while, he noticed that her breathing had steadied. Thalia was asleep, her head leaned back against the wall. The obstinacy was gone from her face when she slept. He moved to wake her up, but stopped when he saw the circles under her eyes. Instead, he gathered her up and lifted her off the floor. She stirred and looked at him with a mixture of befuddlement and alarm.

"It's all right," he said. "Get some rest."

He laid her onto his cot, and she turned onto her side, watching him. "Do you think of her, when you see me?" she asked softly.

"What?"

"Do I remind you of your sister?"

He took a long look at her. Moira had been thin like Thalia. Younger, of course, with all the angles and bones but none of the roundness of womanhood to fill her out. She and Thalia shared the same large eyes, though Moira's had been blue.

"If she had been more like you, she might still be alive," he said.

He turned away and rolled his cloak out on the floor. When he looked at Thalia again, her eyes were closed, and her breathing had regained its steady rhythm. Her hands were curled up by her cheeks, and he once again noticed how fragile her frame was.

James wrapped himself in his cloak and blew out the lantern.

*   *   *

She started spending her nights in James's quarters. They didn't necessarily speak much when she came, but she seemed to find comfort in his company, and James found himself waiting for her arrival every night. Sometimes, she would show up after her work was done at the Tavern. Other nights, she appeared much later, disheveled and still wearing her face paint. They never mentioned where she'd been. What was the point? Hamel had taken a liking to her, and she encouraged his advances even as she counted the days until Alvie's return.

More than once, James wondered why he never turned her away, and why he watched her give herself to the nobleman night after night while he himself stayed back. Not that Thalia would have refused James if he'd tried. She'd been willing enough—or resigned enough—that first time. But there was a wrongness to it that stopped him.

After the first night's exhausted slumber, Thalia slept more fitfully, squirming and talking in her sleep. One night she woke up screaming. James covered her mouth so she wouldn't wake the blacksmith's family and held her until she remembered where she was. Gradually, her breathing slowed and her taut muscles relaxed.

"I can't get the feel of him off my skin," she whispered. Her back was to him, and she clutched his arm tight around her, staring out at nothing.

"You don't have to keep returning to him," he said. "Disappear for a few days. Come back when Alvie gets you the poison."

She reached for Tess's chain around her neck, clutching it like a lifeline. "The moment I leave his sight, he'll fix his eyes on someone new. It's only a few more days."

Meanwhile, James looked for customers to buy Alvie's spices. Rand had some connections with merchants, and James knew a few minor noblemen. It was a trick to make plans without arousing suspicion. Gerred had followed through on his plans to pair James, Rand, and Bacchus with different men during their jobs, and these ill-disguised informants used the pairings as an excuse to sniff around the Scorned Maiden even when they weren't working. But despite all this, James had no trouble finding buyers. Everybody wanted forbidden goods. It was just a matter of getting them into the city, and for that, they had a solid plan. The city walls were tall, slightly taller than three men, but scalable. They would bring the goods in at night, out of view of the Red Shields.

Three days before the handoff, James and Rand scouted the city walls. Rand had found a stretch where trees obscured the watchtowers from view. They stood a few paces off the road and surveyed the surroundings.

"Guards come by twice an hour at night," said Rand.

"Plenty of time, then," said James. He put his shoulder next to the wall and looked to the watchtower. He sometimes glimpsed the guards on duty when the wind stirred the trees, but in the cover of night, they'd be completely hidden. On the opposite side of the wall, he could hear the murmurs of a crowd. "What's on the other side?"

"Shops. They should be empty."

"Good. Let's try scaling it tonight."

There was a sound of boots on gravel. The two of them rushed to the road just in time to see Gerred come around the bend. The guildleader approached slowly, eyes taking in everything—the walls, the rope in James's hand.

"James, Rand," said Gerred with false friendliness. "I heard talk that you might be here."

James and Rand exchanged a look. It was too late to lie. "We all have our side pursuits, Gerred," said James. "It has nothing to do with you. You have my word."

"Your word?" Gerred's tone was still mild, though there was a dangerous glint in his eye. "I expect openness from you. None of this skulking around doing who knows what. You owe me that much."

"We owe Clevon a great deal," said Rand. James shot Rand a warning look. It was unlike him to lose control. But though Rand's face was flushed, he seemed to be reining himself in.

Only a slight hardening in Gerred's expression acknowledged the insult. "Don't be ungrateful, boys," said Gerred. "Don't take what you have for granted."

Chapter Six

RAND'S REMARK ABOUT Clevon had been a mistake. Few things threatened Gerred more than a comparison to his predecessor. But what was done was done.

When Bacchus heard what had happened, he wanted to ditch the plan and attack Gerred. In the end, though, James and Rand prevailed with a more cautious approach. Gerred didn't trust them, but he was a careful planner and slow to act, and they only had three more days until the handoff. So they laid low and kept their routines the same, doing their best not to push Gerred to action.

In the meantime, James inspected Thalia's jewelry. He picked a pair of two matched silver pins as long as her hand. He filed one to a sharp point and left the other one blunt.

"Coat the blunted one with poison and leave the sharp one clean," he said. "This way, you won't poison yourself if your hairpin grazes your scalp. When you're ready to use them, pull them out together. Get used to holding them like this." He pressed them into her palm so that the sharpened pin protruded slightly farther than the poisoned one. "From here, aim for the throat, just as you did with the dagger."

She did as he instructed, slowly angling the hairpins toward his neck. With the fluid motion of habit, James intercepted her hand and grasped the base of her palm, slowing and guiding her motion until the sides of the hairpins pressed cool against his throat. Their eyes met.

"Are you sure you want to do this?" he asked. "You could forget about Hamel. Come with us when we leave."

Indecision flashed across her face, but then she shook her head. "I can't." When she saw his frustration, she gave a wan smile. "Who knows? Perhaps I can kill him and escape."

He stayed silent, biting back words. "Perhaps," he said finally.

She looked into his eyes, silently acknowledging the doubts he hadn't said. Then she took his face in her hands, drawing it down toward her own. Tentatively, almost shyly, she kissed him on the edge of his jawline, his lower lip, the corners of his eyes. Then she stepped back.

He allowed his gaze to roam over her, from her pleading eyes to the curve of her cheeks. He saw her collarbone, the hollow at the base of her throat, her breasts beneath her gown. She was completely still except for the rising and falling of her chest. There was no calculation in her expression, just an acceptance of whatever he would give.

James let out a breath he hadn't known he'd been holding and pulled her close.

*   *   *

The night before the handoff, James, Rand, and Bacchus ate at the Scorned Maiden. Hamel was there as well, with Thalia at his side. James sat with Rand and Bacchus at their usual table, keeping his back to Hamel and Thalia so he wouldn't see them together. His friends must have noticed Thalia's comings and goings from James's quarters by now, just as they had noticed her growing favor with Lord Hamel. They didn't ask any questions, and James offered no explanation.

Gerred came in after the dancing finished, flanked by two of his men. James saw him first and signaled to Rand and Bacchus. The guildmaster planted his feet just inside the door, face dark, and swept his gaze over the room. Then he took a meandering path, first dropping by Hamel's table to say his greetings before approaching the three of them.

"It's the trade caravans, is it?" said Gerred. There was no pretense of friendliness this time.

"Fixing to pick up some extra coin? Buy yourself some allies?"

So Gerred's spies earned their pay after all. "Nothing like that, Gerred," James told him. "The extra coin, yes, but it's for our own purposes. Nothing to do with you."

Bacchus spat on the ground. "If we wanted to give you trouble, we wouldn't have to buy help to get it done."

Gerred's face reddened. Bacchus shifted his weight imperceptibly, and Gerred's eyes flickered toward the movement.

"You really want to bring out weapons, Bacchus?" Gerred's voice was dangerously low.

Bacchus shrugged. "I in't doing anything if you don't." All around them was the buzz of the crowd. The tavern's other patrons were oblivious to their conversation.

"I told you, Gerred," said James. "We've no interest in taking what's yours. We're taking the coin and leaving the city. You can have the Guild."

Gerred fell silent, and James loosened his dagger from his bindings. Out of the corner of his eye, he saw Rand doing the same. Three of them, against Gerred's three. The room was cramped and lit only by a few lanterns, which would complicate things, but they'd always chosen the corner table because it was easier to defend.

Meanwhile, Gerred was still looking at him with suspicion. "Is that really it?" he asked.

"I swear that's all there is."

Gerred turned slowly and walked away. Before James could let out a breath, Gerred passed by Hamel's table and yanked Thalia out of her chair. She cried out in surprise. James jumped to his feet, but Gerred's knife was already to her throat. "You really think I'm simple-minded enough to believe a story like that?" The side doors slammed open, and more of Gerred's crew rushed in. The room echoed with chairs scraping back as people realized what was happening.

Lord Hamel's voice cut through the crowd. "What is this, Gerred?" The nobleman jerked his head, and two brawny men that James recognized as Hamel's bodyguards advanced on the guildleader.

Gerred backed up, pulling Thalia with him. "Your dancing lass has been helping some of my men undermine the Guild."

James felt a brief wave of relief that Gerred didn't know about Thalia's own plans.

"I've no interest in your petty politics," snapped Hamel. "Don't harm her."

Gerred gave Hamel a disbelieving look. "Are you really that attached to her, Steffen? There's plenty of others. I'll give you the next month's jobs for free."

Hamel turned an eye on Gerred, intrigued. "It's that important to you?" he asked. Thalia stood completely still, rigid beneath the assassin's blade.

"Two months. Just don't interfere," growled Gerred, pulling Thalia more tightly to him.

"Fine," said Hamel. He stepped back, dusting off his hands. Thalia's only reaction was a tightening in her jaw.

Gerred nodded. "I owe you." The guildleader turned his attention back to James, Rand, and Bacchus.

The three of them moved closer together. As Bacchus pulled their table in front of them to make a partial barricade,

James took a quick inventory. Ten men, all loyal to Gerred. There was no way they could fight their way out unscathed. Though the idea of negotiating with Gerred turned his stomach, they had to consider it.

"What do you want from us?" he asked Gerred.

"I want you out of the way." He was smug, now that he had the upper hand.

James gritted his teeth. "That's what you would have gotten, Gerred. I told you, we're leaving."

Gerred's expression hardened. "No more lies, James. I've had enough trouble from you." The circle around them tightened.

"Think, Gerred. Do you really want it to come to this?" James said quickly. "You know we won't die easily. This could be a costly fight for you, and a pointless one, if we're telling the truth."

"And I suppose you want me to take you at your word."

"Let the lass go," said James. "The four of us will leave the city tonight. No lives lost. You can march us out the gate if you want." Next to him, Bacchus gave James an incredulous look, but James ignored him.

Gerred narrowed his eyes, but he didn't give the order to attack. James waited, desperately hoping that Gerred's pride wouldn't override his usual caution.

Finally, Gerred spat on the ground. "You leave now. If we see you back in Forge, we kill you on sight."

"Rand? Bacchus?" James said without taking his eyes off Gerred's men.

There was a long silence. "Fine," growled Rand. Next to him, Bacchus made a sound that James decided to take as assent. He looked to Thalia. There was a blazing look in her eyes that he couldn't interpret.

Gerred nodded to his men, and the circle widened a half step. James stepped slowly forward, his blade in his hand, every muscle tense. "Release the lass too."

Slowly, Gerred loosened his grip. Thalia took one step forward, then another. Her eyes locked on James, and they were filled with regret.

"Thalia—" he said.

Before he finished saying her name, the girl spun on her heel and ran for Lord Hamel. The first bodyguard to block her way fell back, clutching at his face as a knife flashed in Thalia's hand. She was turning again to Hamel when the second bodyguard grabbed her hair, pulled her backwards, and thrust a knife between her shoulder blades. Thalia gasped and sank to the floor, her eyes fixed on Hamel's face. The nobleman stared back and wiped off his arm where her blood had splattered.

Bacchus acted first, grabbing the lamp off the table and throwing its contents at one group of assassins as he kicked the table toward the others. The oil caught fire as it fell and spread across the floor. As assassins batted out flames and Gerred yelled orders, James sprang around the fire toward Hamel. The nobleman's bodyguards closed protectively around him, but James dropped to a crouch in front of Thalia. She was pale and gasping, with blood spurting through her knife wound.

"Come on, James," Rand yelled, dragging him to his feet. Rand reached to pick up Thalia, but James pushed him aside and scooped her up himself. Bacchus waved them out the door and guarded their retreat, knife raised in a menacing crouch as he backed out last.

No one pursued them. There were shouts of Red Shields, so perhaps Gerred's crew had scattered rather than risk capture. When it was clear they weren't being followed, James laid Thalia on the ground. The bleeding had slowed. She was in shock, though when she looked at James, her eyes took a momentary focus. Her lips moved, and James leaned closer to hear.

"Kill him for me," she said.

And then she was too weak to say anything else.

Chapter Seven

ALVIE WAITED IN the shadow of his wagon train, arms folded across his chest. Today was one of those days when he felt the weight of his years. His back ached from setting up camp, and everything felt heavy.

He hadn't been surprised by the news when it came through the rumor mills. Everyone who'd known Thalia had been preparing to hear it for a while. The girl had been headstrong and fiercely loyal to her sister. These were characteristics one couldn't afford to indulge when dealing with people like Hamel.

There was a rustle in the trees, and the young assassin came around a wagon. He was vigilant as he came into the circle, his eyes sweeping in all directions. Alvie imagined that James looked more tired than when they'd last met. His eyes were colder.

The assassin didn't waste time on niceties. "You've heard by now?" he asked.

"Enough," said Alvie. "I'll relay the news to her home caravan. Let them claim their right to avenge her, if they so choose."

"They didn't avenge her sister," James said. There might have been a hint of disdain in his voice.

"True," Alvie conceded. "But don't blame them for Thalia's death. They loved the girls like their own daughters, and their decision not to go up against one of Forge's top noblemen does not diminish that."

"Whether they loved her or not is of no consequence to me. But they need not worry about vengeance. I'll take responsibility for it," James said.

Alvie believed him, the way he spoke. "You'll strike against Hamel?" said Alvie. "There will be consequences, if I understand how your city functions."

"I know the risks."

It was on Alvie's tongue to ask why only now, after the girl's death, was James finally willing to go against the nobleman. But one look at the assassin's face convinced him to keep the question to himself. "Why did you help her?" Alvie asked instead. "If you knew she'd likely fail?" He was careful not to inject any anger into his voice. The time for anger was past, and Alvie simply wanted to know.

James looked warily at Alvie, but seemed to sense that the trader meant no harm. "Risk is everywhere. Only the nobles have the luxury of a long easy life. Justice, vengeance, the ability to carve out your own fate instead of being herded like an animal. Sometimes it's worth dying for."

"I take it that you were close to Thalia, then?" Alvie asked.

"It doesn't matter now." That was probably as close a man like him would ever come to admitting love.

One of the horses neighed and they both looked to the sound, but there was no one else nearby. When the assassin turned back to their conversation, his tone was matter-of-fact.

"I'm afraid the city is too unstable now for our old plan," said James. "If you can wait. . ."

Alvie waved away James's concerns. "I've waited years. A few months won't hurt."

"I appreciate it. Though I do want some goods from you today."

"Certainly." Alvie turned to his wagons. "What'll it be?"

"Lizard skin venom. Three vials." Perhaps Alvie's surprise showed, because James continued, "I understand you were bringing some for her."

Alvie swung back toward the assassin, regarding him now with interest. "I do have a few vials, but it's expensive."

James palmed something from his belt pouch. "I trust this will be enough."

There was just the slightest hesitation, a possessive last clench of the assassin's fist before he opened his hand to reveal an exquisite gold chain. The craftsmanship was undeniable in the delicacy of the leaf-shaped links. James looked away as Alvie inspected it.

"This will be more than enough," Alvie said. "And I can supply you with more, should you run out. Do you have much need for venoms?"

And suddenly there was a glint in James's eye. "I do."

Epilogue

IT HAPPENED QUICKLY. The magistrates barely investigated the deaths because they involved the city's lowlifes, violent criminals whose deaths were not widely mourned. But there were many. One night, eleven bodies were left by the river. Their faces were purple, their extremities gray. Poison.

When Lord Hamel heard the news, he flew into a rage. But then Hamel disappeared too. His bodyguards were discovered a few days later, throats cleanly slit. Hamel's body, when it finally turned up, showed signs of a more lingering death, as drawn out as his bodyguards' had been quick. A silver hairpin was carefully wedged under each of the nobleman's fingernails.

Though Hamel was the only wallhugger to be harmed, other nobles also seemed out of sorts. More astute servants noted that these noblemen's enemies were no longer terrorized by thugs. Whoever had been doing their dirty work was no longer in their employ.

After a few weeks, the violence died down, and the city returned to normal. Better than normal, in fact. Crime in the city plummeted. Red Shields were no longer called on as often to enforce the law. And as the Palace officials each tried to take the credit for this turn of fortune, they were unaware of the rumors circling in the taverns that a new leader had taken over the Assassins Guild, who had defeated his rivals so soundly that none remained. Those whispers circulated in the city, unnoticed by the Palace, for a very long time.

Note from Livia

THANK YOU FOR taking the time to read *Poison Dance*! I hope you enjoyed it. If you did, I hope you will:

1. **Write an online review.** They really help get the word out about the book!
2. **Check out** *Midnight Thief*. James was originally conceived as a key character in my young adult novel *Midnight Thief*. You can read the first chapter on the next page.
3. **Join my mailing list.** I keep a low volume mailing list to let people know about new releases and special sales. You can sign up at http://liviablackburne.com.

For more *Poison Dance* related tidbits, I've posted some deleted scenes and behind-the-scenes blog posts at http://liviablackburne.com. Or, if you're reading the paperback version, just go to the end of the book.

Midnight Thief Excerpt

GROWING UP ON *Forge's streets has taught Kyra how to stretch a coin. And when that's not enough, her uncanny ability to scale walls and bypass guards helps her take what she needs.*

But when the leader of the Assassins Guild offers Kyra a lucrative job, she hesitates. She knows how to get by on her own, and she's not sure she wants to play by his rules. But he's persistent—and darkly attractive—and Kyra can't quite resist his pull.

Tristam of Brancel is a young Palace knight on a mission. After his best friend is brutally murdered by Demon Riders, a clan of vicious warriors who ride bloodthirsty wildcats, Tristam vows to take them down. But as his investigation deepens, he finds his efforts thwarted by a talented thief, one who sneaks past Palace defenses with uncanny ease.

When a fateful raid throws Kyra and Tristam together, the two enemies realize that their best chance at survival—and vengeance— might be to join forces. And as their loyalties are tested to the breaking point, they learn a startling secret about Kyra's past that threatens to reshape both their lives.

In her arresting debut novel, Livia Blackburne creates a captivating world where intrigue prowls around every corner—and danger is a way of life.

*   *   *

Chapter 1

This job could kill her.

Kyra peered off the ledge, squinting at the cobblestone four stories below. A false step in the darkness would be deadly, and even if she survived the fall, Red Shields would finish her off. She stared a few moments more before forcing her gaze back up. The time for second thoughts was past. Now she just needed to keep moving.

The jump ahead was two body lengths long, so Kyra backed away from the ledge. Ten steps, then she drew a breath and sprinted forward. She pushed off just before the drop, clearing a gap of three strides before softening her body for the landing. There was a slap of soft leather on stone as she hit the next ledge. The impact sent a wave of vibrations through the balls of her feet, and Kyra touched a hand to the wall for balance.

Too hard, and too loud.

Silently cursing her clumsiness, Kyra scanned the grounds, looking for anyone who might have heard her. If she squinted, she could make out faint outlines of buildings around her—some as high as her ledge, some even taller. The pathways below were lined with torches that flickered, casting shadows that played tricks with her vision. Since she couldn't trust her eyes, she listened. Other than the wind blowing across her ears, the night was silent, and Kyra relaxed. Tucking away a stray lock of hair, she set off, dashing deeper into the compound.

Two days ago, a man had come to the Drunken Dog, introducing himself as James and asking for Kyra by name. He'd moved with a deliberate confidence, and his gaze had swept over the room, evaluating and dismissing each of its occupants. When Kyra had finally approached him, James laid out an unusual offer. There was a ruby in the Palace compound. He wanted her to fetch it for him, and he was willing to pay.

"The Palace is guarded tight," Kyra had told him. "If you want jewels, you'll better get them elsewhere."

"This ruby's got sentimental value," he'd replied. Kyra didn't consider herself the most astute judge of character. But she also wasn't an idiot, and she'd swallow her grappling hook before she'd believe that this man would do *anything* for sentimental reasons. The pay he offered was good, though, and the job an intriguing challenge. The Palace was a far cry from the rich man's houses Kyra usually raided, with their handful of sentries guarding two or three floors. The Palace's massive buildings were patrolled by so many guards, it was impossible to walk the grounds undetected. Rumor had it that even the rooftops were closely watched.

Which was why Kyra was neither on the ground nor on the rooftops. Instead, she balanced on a ledge outside a fourth-floor window, darting from shadow to shadow. The moon had not yet risen, and darkness concealed her from the Red Shields below. Unfortunately, it also hid the ledges from her own sight; the boundary between stone and air was easy to miss. From time to time, she slid a foot out to check her position, tracing her toe along the edge to fix the border in her mind.

Yes, she could die tonight. But as Kyra crept through the darkness, her doubts faded against the excitement of a challenging job. Those who knew her understood her skills. They knew she had no fear of heights and never lost her balance. But not even Flick, the closest thing to an older brother she had, understood the sheer joy that came over her every time she raced through the night. There was something about the way the darkness forced her to rely on her other senses, the way her body rose to the challenge. Her limbs silently promised her she would not fall, and by now she knew she could trust them.

The buildings across the path gave way to a courtyard with three trees, and Kyra slowed her pace, counting windows as she passed. The seventh from the southwest corner, James had said. These outer palaces were guest rooms for country noblemen visiting the Council. They were built securely but emphasized comfort more heavily than the fortresslike inner compound. And thus, they had glass windows instead of shutters, making it easy to see that the bedroom inside was dark. A minute fiddling with the latch, and the pane swung open on greased hinges. There was a shape on the bed, snoring in the loud and punctuated way of men who had indulged too much in rich food and drink. Kyra wondered for a moment what it would be like to get fat, to eat so much, and work so little. No matter. Tonight, the nobleman would share some of his bounty.

She started with a dresser next to the bed, coaxing open the top drawer. Silk caught the dry skin of her fingertips. Apparently, the nobleman had a penchant for embroidered silk handkerchiefs. Not the jewelry box she sought, but Kyra took one and slipped it into her belt pouch. After checking the rest of the dresser, she moved to the desk. The latch gave easily to her pick, but there was nothing inside but documents and seals.

The sleeping nobleman shifted, and Kyra dropped to the floor. He rolled over, snorting loudly before his breathing once again settled. Kyra counted ten breaths, then went to the chest, taking care with the hefty cover. The top layer was fabric. Soon, she was up to her elbows in velvet night-robes, but still no ruby. If there were a jewelry box, it almost certainly would have been in the dresser or the chest. James had assured her that the nobleman wasn't the type to hide his jewelry. Could he have been mistaken?

She combed the room again, feeling along the floors and walls for trapdoors, even running her hands over the bed's thin mattress. Still nothing. Kyra bit her lip. The moon was rising, a thin crescent above the horizon that announced the coming dawn. She'd already stayed too long. Taking one last glance around the room, she crept back out the window.

Getting out was harder than coming in. Her limbs were slow from a night without sleep, and her nerves were frayed from being so long on her guard. By the time Kyra reached the meeting spot two blocks outside the Palace, the sky was visibly lighter, and she was in a considerably worse mood.

Two men awaited her at the street corner. They hadn't seen her yet, and she took a moment to study them. The first was solidly built, with a stubborn jaw and brown hair curled close to his head—Flick. When Kyra had first told him about the job, he'd listed all the reasons she should refuse, from the dangers within the Palace to his suspicions about James. Her friend's arguments had been more reasonable than Kyra cared to admit, but by then she'd already decided. Since Flick couldn't dissuade her from going, he'd insisted on escorting James. The two men had watched her cross the wall a few hours earlier, and now they awaited her return. Kyra felt a twinge of guilt when she saw the tense set of Flick's shoulders. He'd been worried.

Behind Flick, Kyra recognized James. He was slimmer but taller, with pale coloring and a wiry, athletic build. He exuded confidence, studying everything around him with languid readiness. His expression was impossible to read.

Both men's eyes flickered to her hands as she came closer, then to her belt.

"It in't there," she said, answering their unspoken question. Perhaps her voice was sharper than it should have been, but she was tired.

There was a brief silence as the two men digested her news. Finally, James spoke. "What do you mean?"

"I flipped the whole room—the dresser, desk, the chest at the foot of the bed. No jewelry box."

"You searched the entire room?" James raised an eyebrow.

Kyra spat on the ground. "Look, unless he sleeps with the rock in his smallclothes, it wasn't there."

"Maybe you went to the wrong place."

There was a hint of derision in his voice, and it galled Kyra. Trying hard to control a flush of anger, she reached into her belt pouch for the handkerchief she'd taken from the noble's dresser. She flicked it at James, who snatched it out of the air with surprising quickness.

"This handkerchief's got the fatpurse's initials embroidered on it. See if it matches your mark."

Kyra made no effort to hide her frustration as James inspected the embroidery. Payment for the job depended on handing over the jewel, so she'd taken a long and dangerous night's work for nothing. She felt a hand on her shoulder. Flick, knowing her temper, was silently warning her not to push anything too far. Kyra gritted her teeth. James studied the handkerchief, after a while not even looking at it, but through it. Finally, he looked up, and his demeanor abruptly changed.

"Very well," he said, voice now smooth and agreeable. "Mayhap he didn't bring the stone to the Palace." James untied a pouch from his belt and tossed it at Kyra, who almost didn't react quickly enough to catch it. "That's the agreed-upon price, plus some extra. I believe this will cover your effort."

Without another word, he turned and walked away.

To be notified when Midnight Thief *releases, sign up for my email list at http://liviablackburne.com. (Expected publication July 8, 2014.)*

Acknowledgements

IT TRULY TAKES a village to create a book. And since *Poison Dance* was my first self published work, this was doubly true.

Since I usually write about teenage girls, writing a story from James's point of view did not come naturally to me. I credit Barry Eisler's John Rain books, Alex Bledsoe's Eddie Lacrosse Series, and Dan Simmons's Endymion books with providing me with good models for badass male characters.

Thanks to my alpha readers Amitha Knight, Rachal Aronson, Emily Terry, and Jennifer Barnes for early encouragement and sniffing out of plot holes, and beta readers Coral Frazer, Anna Redmond, and Jessica Corra for looking over the completed drafts.

My editor Shannon Barefield offered fantastic insight into my story, and copy editor Mary Thompson put the finishing touches on the manuscript. Then proofreaders Letty Kwok, Joe Moran, Christine Hahn, Beata Shih, Bethany Lau, Tracie Chuang, and Cassie Eng were kind enough to give the book one more read through.

Thanks as well to my cover artist Lauren Kudo for a beautiful design.

The learning curve for digital publishing is quite steep, but I was lucky to have writer friends who've walked the path before me and offered valuable advice: Barry Eisler, Joanna Penn, CJ Lyons, David Vandagriff, Moses Siregar, and the very talented and generous authors of Marie Force's self publishing loop.

Poison Dance is a tie-in story to my young adult novel *Midnight Thief*, which is published through Disney Hyperion. Many thanks to my Disney editor Rotem Moscovich and the rest of the Disney-Hyperion team for being open to experimentation, and to my agent Jim McCarthy for facilitating everything.

And last but not least, thank you to my husband, who doesn't roll his eyes *too* often when I ramble on about James and Thalia. And a big thank you to my parents. To my mom, for buying me those first books, and to my dad for always having good business advice.

Deleted Scenes

HERE ARE TWO scenes that I wrote for Poison Dance but ultimately decided to cut. They show James getting his revenge on Gerred and Lord Hamel. In the end, I decided it was better to leave these moments up to the reader's imagination. I wanted the moment of Thalia's death to be a transformation for James, the point at which he becomes a mystery. But for those who are curious, here they are.

* * *

Scene 1: James and Gerred

Gerred strode down the narrow alleyway. Beside him, three of his men hurried to keep up.

"No sign of any of them?" he said, making sure the displeasure in his voice was obvious. It had been a mistake not to kill James and his supporters earlier. He should have picked them off quietly when he first suspected them of working behind his back. But he wouldn't make the same mistake twice.

"They've abandoned their own lodgings," said his man Darron. "They also know well enough to stay away from the Scorned Maiden. In a city this size, it could take weeks to find them. That's assuming they even stayed."

"We find them. We kill them," said Gerred. "No excuses. I want everybody after them until this is done. We'll go over the new plans when everyone is here." They rounded the corner and came to the door of an empty storehouse. An assassin named Bors reached for the doorknob, but Gerred pulled him back.

"Where are the door guards?" he asked.

His men exchanged glances, and then slowly drew their blades as the realization dawned on them. Gerred looked at Darron and jerked his head to the door. Darron nodded and edged closer, finally kicking the door open when he was close enough.

Silence inside. And as their eyes adjusted to see the bodies through the doorway, the smell of blood wafted out to meet them. Blood, and something else. Darron led the way in, followed by Bors while Gerred and the last man Swinton stood guard at the door.

Bors' voice drifted out. "They're gone."

"How many dead?" Gerred asked.

"Six."

Motioning for Swinton to stay, Gerred ducked inside. As Bors had reported, six of his men lay lifeless on the ground. The body closest to him was cleanly run through. Gerred continued to the next one. Barth, one of his best. He was surprised that Barth would've succumbed this easily. Gerred knelt to take a closer look. The body bore some superficial wounds. A shallow cut on the chest, a graze along his arm. But how did he die?

Outside, Swinton yelled, then swore. By the time the rest of them rushed outside, Swinton was leaning against the wall, cradling a wounded arm. Gerred gripped his blade and scanned the shadows. "Who was it?"

"Bacchus," he spat. "Bastard took a swipe at me and ran away." Swinton's breathing was labored. As the wounded man sank to his knees, Gerred suddenly understood. He hauled

Swinton to his feet and pried open his eyelid. "Look at me." As he suspected, Swinton's pupils could not focus.

Gerred let go of Swinton and looked around more urgently. "If you see them, don't let them cut you," he said to his surviving men. "Not even a graze, hear me?"

A slight movement of air, and the soft thud of someone landing behind him. Gerred spun to face his attacker, but not before he felt a slash across his back.

∗   ∗   ∗

Scene 2: James and Hamel

Fletcher stood at attention in the corridor, doing his best to stay expressionless as the sounds of his employer's rage drifted out through the doorway. Hamel was well known for his temper, but this episode was extreme even for him.

"Think this has anything to do with his city friends?" asked his fellow bodyguard Tomlin.

Fletcher shrugged. His stitches still hurt when he spoke, so he preferred to be silent in the absence of anything consequential to say. It was his own fault, he supposed, letting his guard down around that girl. He should've known she might have a knife, especially since they had taken one off her that first night.

"I'll wager it is," Tomlin prattled on. "We in't been to the city for a week. Something's gone wrong."

There was a sound from around the corner, like metal dragging on stone. The two of them exchanged a glance.

"I'll go look," said Tomlin.

A moment after he disappeared around the corner, Fletcher heard a muffled grunt. Then nothing.

"Tomlin?" Fletcher drew his short sword and walked to investigate.

He didn't realize that someone was behind him until he felt the blade at his neck. Fletcher froze. A voice spoke in his ear.

"I have no personal grievance with you, but your job puts you in the way. I'll make this quick."

A burning pain across his neck, and then warmth. As darkness closed in around him, the voice spoke again.

"My time with your employer, however, will be a more drawn out affair."

Operation Chest Hair

MY USUAL GENRE is young adult fiction with girl protagonists. So when I decided to write a story from James's point of view, I needed some help making it realistic. Here are two blog posts I wrote in which I analyzed books with tough male characters to see if I could learn that type of voice.

* * *

Operation Chest Hair Part I: Attraction

I write about teenage girls. That's my comfort zone, but I recently got an idea for a story from a man's point of view.

This made me nervous. I'd written boys before (not without difficulty), but this new story was about a Man's Man. You know, the kind of guy that drinks black coffee and crushes rocks with his bare hands. To be honest, I didn't know if I had the balls to pull it off. And thus, Operation Chest Hair was born, in which I analyze Man Books in an attempt to raise my testosterone level.

I had two criteria for books to analyze. First, the book had to be narrated by a man. Second, it had to be written by a man (a manly man, if you will) to ensure accuracy. On my dorm room bookshelf, I had two books that fit: Barry Eisler's *Rain Fall*, about half-Japanese assassin John Rain, and Alex Bledsoe's *The Sword-Edged Blonde*, about freelance sword jockey Eddie Lacrosse. Now I know that men are complicated, multidimensional creatures, but for the sake of analysis, I needed to focus on specific themes.

Today's topic: women (an important topic for men).

I wanted to see how these characters looked at a potential love interest. To narrow things down further, I focused on early encounters when they're getting to know the gal. **So when you're ready, grab a beer, slather some Rogaine on your chest, and let's dive right in.**

[Actually, one more clarification. I want to be clear here that I'm not attempting some kind of complex analysis of the male psyche. This is a writerly exercise focused on picking up aspects of voice from a certain type of male character in the specific situation of meeting the future love interest, so please don't read more into this than I intended . . .]

Okay, now we really can begin.

In *Rain Fall*, John Rain first sees jazz pianist Midori when she performs.

I watched Midori's face as she took up her post at the piano. She looked to be in her mid 30's and had straight, shoulder length hair so black it seemed to glisten in the overhead light. She was wearing a short sleeve pullover, as black as her hair, the smooth white skin of her arms and neck appearing almost to float beside it. I tried to see her eyes but could catch only a glimpse in the shadows cast by the overhead light. She had framed them in eyeliner, I saw, but other than that she was unadorned. Confident enough not to trouble herself. Not that she needed to. She looked good and must have been aware of it.

Later on, they meet and get a chance to talk. Here's how Rain describes her this second time.

For the first time, I was in a position to notice her body. She was slender and long limbed, perhaps a legacy from her father . . . Her shoulders were broad, a lovely counterpart to a long and graceful neck. Her breasts were small, and, I couldn't help but notice, shapely beneath her sweater. The skin on the exposed portion of her chest was beautiful: smooth and white, framed by the contrast of the black V-neck.

What about Eddie Lacrosse? He first sees Liz from afar as she's fighting off three bandits.

In the center of the triangle stood a slender, redhaired girl, as tall as me though with that willowy quality so many country girls possess. She had short hair and was dressed like a man, which actually made her look more feminine. But this was certainly no helpless maiden.

After he helps her in the fight, he takes a closer look.

Then she faced me, and I got my first close look at her. She had wide shoulders and the kind of trim narrow body that spoke of hard muscle beneath her baggy clothes. A deep scar cut through her right eyebrow and touched her hairline, where a streak of white sprang from it.

Here's what I noticed.

1. The men are looking at both the woman's face and body.

So it's interesting. In both books the guy sees the woman from far away at first. Then she moves closer, and in both books, the guy makes a point of taking a closer look.

In terms of physical description, it's very precise language, often mentioning specific body parts (long and graceful neck, small breasts, wide shoulders, hard muscle). Which brings me to point two.

2. The men are looking at clothing in relation to the body.

For example, Midori's black clothes contrast with her skin. Liz's clothes make her look more feminine. And sometimes, it seems like the guys are more interested in looking *through* the clothes than at them. :-)

I was curious about how this compares to YA heroines, so I grabbed a pile of books off my shelf. It seems like teenage girls are much more about the face. A few do mention the guy's body, but it's very general language, usually referring to build.

For example, Elisa from *The Girl of Fire and Thorns* gushes about her King Alejandro's friendly smile and beautiful teeth. Aly from *Trickster's Choice* spends four sentences describing Nawat's face and then mentions that he is "6 feet tall, with a wiry build." Cate from *Born Wicked* sees Finn's freckles and notes that he's no longer scrawny. As for her other suitor Paul, he's taller, has a mustache and beard, and "looks quite the gentleman in his frock coat." Katsa from *Graceling* notices Po's gold earrings, his rings, his dark hair, and his eyes. The only allusion to his body is that the neck of his shirt is open.

I was curious as to whether the focus on face rather than body were more because of the YA heroines' age or their gender. So I picked up Karen Marie Moning's *Darkfever*. Darkfever is an adult romance, and the Mackayla Lane is no innocent flower. What does she notice in the first meeting between her and Jericho Barrons?

He didn't just occupy space; he saturated it. The room had been full of books before, now was full of him. About thirty, six foot two or three, he had dark hair, golden skin, and dark eyes. His features were strong, chiseled. I couldn't pinpoint his nationality ... He wore an elegant, dark gray Italian suit, a crisp white shirt, and a muted map patterned tie. He wasn't handsome. That was too common a word. He was intensely masculine. He was sexual. He attracted. There was an omnipresent carnality about him, his dark eyes, and his full mouth, in the way he stood. He was the kind of man I wouldn't flirt with in a million years.

So there's certainly nothing shy or innocent about this description, but even Mac describes the Jericho's body with less detail than his face or even his clothes. (Note also, that Cate from Born Wicked also describes Paul's frock coat and other clothing in detail.)

It's not like these women never look at a guy's body if it's there in front of them. In Graceling, there's a delightful scene in which Po takes his shirt off and Katsa makes a heroic effort not to gawk, and Mac gets quite a few eyefuls in the Fever series. But in general, there's less of an effort to develop x-ray vision.

There was one notable exception to this trend: Bella Swan from *Twilight*. Bella notices early on that Edward's forearm is "surprisingly hard and muscular." In later scenes, she gushes over his "sculpted, incandescent chest," and his "scintillating arms." Does this have something to do with Twilight's mysterious ability to drive teenage girls into a hormonal craze? Hmmm . . .

Okay, moving on . . .

3. Both John Rain and Eddie LaCrosse specifically mention the woman's attractiveness early on. And not just that she's good looking, but also whether or not she knows it.

" . . . she was unadorned. Confident enough not to trouble herself. Not that she needed to. She looked good and must have been aware of it." – Rain Fall

"She was cute rather than pretty, and I just bet she knew that and it bugged the hell out of her." -TSEB

YA heroines were less straightforward about physical attraction. Elisa does mention that Alejandro is beautiful, and Bella definitely notices Edward. Other heroines, however, simply note a pleasant face or don't mention that the guy is attractive at all (though it's implied). As to whether or not he knows he's good looking, the closest I found was from Graceling.

Then he raised his eyebrows and hair, and his mouth shifted into a hint of a smirk. He nodded at her, just barely, and it released her from her spell. Cocky, she thought. Cocky and arrogant, this one, and that was all there was to make of him.

And one last observation.

4. Both men mention how the woman's attractiveness affects and/or distracts them.

"What the hell is wrong with you? I thought. You've got nothing to do with her or her father. She's attractive, it's getting to you. Okay. But drop it." -Rain Fall

"Yes, she was attractive. And yes, I noticed, and yes, it had been a while for me. But besides the fact that she was not very encouraging (she insisted we always sleep with the fire between us), I just wasn't motivated that way." -TSEB

So in this case, I do see similar things happening with the YA heroines. Bella falls all over herself over Edward's beauty. Katsa is distracted by Po's eyes, and Elisa by Alejandro's good looks. However, the girls are usually not really thinking about whether they'll make a move. Could this be due to the social script of the women as the pursued rather than the pursuer?

So here ends my somewhat haphazard sampling of men and women in romance, and I'd now like to enlist your help. **What do you think? Do you have any supporting examples, or counter examples, on your bookshelves?**

*   *   *

Operation Chest Hair Part II: Grief

Spoiler warning: Major spoilers for *The Sword Edged Blonde* by Alex Bledsoe, *The Rise of Endymion* by Dan Simmons, *Rain Fall* by Barry Eisler, *Lioness Rampant* by Tamora Pierce, *Plain Kate* by Erin Bow, and *The Girl of Fire and Thorns* by Rae Carson.

Wow, time flies. It's been over six months since the last installment of Operation Chest Hair.

Operation Chest Hair started when I had a story idea with a male point-of-view (POV) character. And not just any any old guy—a manly man. The rugged, tough type that wrestles grizzly bears and uses undiluted tabasco sauce for mouthwash. A far cry from my teenage girls I usually write. To train my voice to write such a paragon of masculinity, I've been studying books with manly characters.

My previous article focused on how these man characters respond to the introduction of a love interest. In this article, I want to look at how they deal with grief, and how their reaction to loss compares to YA heroines in similar situations.

As before, I chose to study books with male POV characters that were written by male authors. In each of these books, these male protagonists lost loved ones. How did they react? There was a lot of variation, but I did pick up some tidbits.

1. No crying

First, take a look at these passages where YA heroines mourn their loved ones.

Her eyes burned, but she was cried out. Hopelessly she plucked at his sleeve, wishing she could bring him back. Crying would have helped.
-*Lioness Rampant* by Tamora Pierce

Glad to be alone, Alanna sat and wept, letting the Dragon go at last.
-*Lioness Rampant*

Something flashed through her, surprising her with a sting of tears. She thought it was bewilderment, anger, fear – before she recognized it: grief.
-*Plain Kate* by Erin Bow

I hear a keening sound. High-pitched, wild. I realize it's me ... I can't speak. I'm shaking too badly. The faces of my companions blur as a sharp pain streaks to my temples. Oh God, oh God ... The Godstone warms to my grief.
-*The Girl of Fire and Thorns* by Rae Carson

There's lots of crying and grief here here from the YA heroines. But from the men? Across the board, not a single tear.

So how do the men respond? Let's move on to the next observation.

2. Muted Grief (sometimes)

In two of the books with male characters, I noticed a muted presentation of grief.

In the passage below, John Rain talks to his associate Tatsu, who tells Rain that he must let his lover Midori believe that he's dead.

"You may be tempted to contact her," [Tatsu] continued. "I would advise against this. She believes you are dead."

"Why would she believe that?"

"Because I told her."

"Tatsu," I said, my voice dangerously flat, "Explain yourself." . . .

He paused for a long moment, then looked at me squarely, his eyes resigned. "I deeply regret the pain you feel now. However I am more convinced even than before that I did the right thing in telling her. . . .

I wasn't even surprised Tatsu had put together all the pieces. "She didn't have to know," I heard myself say . . .

I realized, but somehow could not grasp, that Midori had already been made part of my past. It was like a magic trick. Now you see it, now you don't. Now it's real; now it's just a memory.

-Rain Fall by Barry Eisler

Here, John Rain's grief is only hinted at by his "dangerously flat" voice and his confusion. He "hears himself" protest. He tries but "somehow cannot grasp" that Midori is gone. The only pain mentioned in this passage is brought up not by Rain, but by Tatsu when he mentions the "pain you feel now." There's no wallowing in grief here, but because we've been with Rain for the whole book and know his voice, we pick up on these more subtle clues.

In *The Sword-Edged Blonde,* Eddie LaCrosse finds out that his friend Cathy has been murdered. His reaction is a bit stronger. Though he doesn't speak directly about his grief, his worry for his friend shows through in his actions.

The roof of Betty's little not-a-tavern collapsed in a big puff of sparks. My chest was on fire, too, from all that running, and from the agony of realizing Cathy had to be among the dead.
Unless . . .
I had to know. I ran through the village, heedless of the heat and danger. "Cathy!" I yelled. I dodged chickens and goats, free of their pens and frantically seeking shelter or escape. I did not look at the other corpses except to make sure they weren't her.

After he's sure of Cathy's death, however, LaCrosse's grief reaction is also more muted than the YA heroines. I'd describe it as drained.

The only person I buried was Cathy, in a shallow grave with no marker. I found her charred—boiled, really—body still in the metal tub inside one of the ruined buildings . . . The smell was as appalling as it sounds.
At dawn, I returned to Epona's cottage. No horses followed me through the forest. No weird bird sang overhead. The house was exactly as I've left it, but the woman—whoever she'd been—was gone. Perhaps the poisoned wine had driven her into the forest to die. I didn't know, and didn't really care. I considered torching the place, but I'd seen enough destruction to do me for a while.

LaCrosse talks about the apalling smell of corpses, about how he'd seen a lot of destruction, but he doesn't talk explicitly about how sad he is.

The one case where grief was not muted was for Raul Endymion, from Dan Simmon's Hyperion series. He had the most painful loss of all three male characters. Endymion was forced to watch his longtime friend and lover be tortured to death, and his reaction is full-on pain and madness.

I began screaming in my high-g tank, ripping at life support umbilicals and banging the bulkhead with my head and fists, until the water-filled tank was swirling with my blood. I tried tearing at the osmosis mask that covered my face like some parasite sucking away my breath; it would not tear. For a full three hours I screamed and protested, battering myself into a state of semiconsciousness at best, reliving the shared moments with Aenea a thousand times and screaming in agony a thousand times, and then the robot ship injected sleep drugs through the leechlike umbilicals.
-The *Rise of Endymion* by Dan Simmons

3. Reactions of Pain/Anger/Madness

Another thing I noticed was that the male characters reacted to their loss with anger. John Rain's voice, for example, becomes "dangerously flat" when he hears of Tatsuo's deception.

When Eddie Lacrosse hears that Cathy has been murdered, he runs in panic to the city to look for her body. He discovers the man who killed her, and he also responds with anger and battle rage.

My pulse returned to normal, then continued to slow, as panic and horror dissolved into cold soldierly professionalism. I saw no reason to delay any longer. "Did you kill Cathy, too?". . .

I let my jacket fall to the ground. After Eppie's hut, and my mad run, and the heat from the burning village, I was drenched in sweat. Yet inside I was solid ice.
-The *Sword Edged Blonde*

And of course, there's Endymion's violent reaction quoted earlier.

I was curious about whether the young adult heroines exhibited the same anger and wish for revenge.

Plain Kate, when she loses her dear friend Taggle the cat, is angry at the man responsible for Taggle's death, but she also takes his hand in compassion as he lays dying.

[Linay] looked up first at Kate, then Eleanor, and then—blankly—at the clearing sky. "I feel strange," he said. "I think I'm dying."

Kate, with the little body in her arms, answered, "Good. We don't like you." But she knelt beside him and took his raw hand.

-Plain Kate

Interestingly, a few heroines blamed themselves rather than the villain. When Alanna loses her twin brother Thom to the schemes of the evil wizard Roger, this is her reaction.

Alanna didn't know how long she sat, holding Thom's cold hand. She was certain somehow this was all her fault. How was she supposed to live without her other half?

-Lioness Rampant

In the next scene, however, Alanna does become angry.

Rage was replacing her grief. She wanted to act . . .

-Lioness Rampant

In *The Girl of Fire and Thorns*, when an enemy kills Elisa's love Humberto, her first reaction is also to blame herself. Convinced that the Godstone in her navel is the reason her enemies have been hurting her and her friends, she takes a dagger and attempts to cut it from her flesh. After her initial grief, however, Elisa also makes plans for revenge.

Strange that I have been loathe to use a knife on a man. Now, I relish the prospect. "Tomorrow, I kill Trevino."
-*Girl of Fire and Thorns*

So in summary, it appears that both the manly men and YA heroines express anger and a desire for revenge, although the YA heroines' anger was more delayed, and they were more quick to blame themselves.

4. Philosophizing

One thing I didn't expect to find was that two of the male characters processed their loss through philosophical reflection. John Rain has a long interior monologue on the nature of his loss.

I thought about Tatsu. I knew he had done right in telling Midori I was dead . . .
He was right, too, about my loss not being a long-term issue for her. She was young and had a brilliant career opening up right in front of her. When you've known someone only briefly, even if intensely, death comes as a shock, but not a particularly long or deep one. After all, there was no time for the person in question to become woven tightly into the fabric of your life. . . . There were moments with her when I would forget everything I had done, everything I had become. But those moments would never have lasted. I have the product of things I have done, and I know I will always wake up to this conclusion, no matter how beguiling the reverie that precedes the awakening.
-*Rain Fall*

In the case of Raul Endymion, the entire book is his memoir, a vehicle to help him understand what had happened.

We're leaving here, Raul, my darling," she whispered in the darkness last night." Not soon, but as soon as you finish our tale. As soon as you remember it all and understand it all. -Endymion

There was nothing like this in the YA books that I checked. The closest was in Alanna's story. A few weeks after her lover's death, she receives a letter from him (written before his death) telling her he is at peace and explaining that he had found meaning in his upcoming death.

The truth is we never saw death the same (like some other things), so I didn't talk about it with you. All you think of death is ending. To me, it's how a person goes. Dying for important things—that's better than living safe.

I often visited Tortall, though we never met there. The last two times . . . I felt a change . . . If I can protect this beginning, I will have died a Dragon.

So Alanna does find meaning in her lover's death, but he's the one who explains her to her.

I'm not sure if this difference is due to gender or age. The YA heroines are much younger, and perhaps their youth is why they don't process and make sense of their grief this way. Or is it a gender issue?

Now readers, what do you think? Are there differences in how grief is portrayed in men vs. women in literature? If so, are these due to true gender differences or societal expectations?